# GHOST for Sale

# GHOST for Sale

# TERRY DEARY

With illustrations by
**Stefano Tambellini**

Barrington Stoke

First published in 2005 in Great Britain by
Barrington Stoke Ltd
18 Walker Street, Edinburgh, EH3 7LP

www.barringtonstoke.co.uk

This edition first published in 2015

This edition based on *Ghost for Sale*, published by
Barrington Stoke in 1999

Text © 2005 Terry Deary
Illustrations © 2015 Stefano Tambellini

A CIP catalogue record for this book is available
from the British Library upon request

ISBN: 978-1-78112-518-2

Printed in China by Leo

# Contents

# Streatley, Berkshire, England

# 1937

Ghosts are scary.  They shock and terrify anyone who sees them.  So why do so many people try to see a ghost?  Lots of people love to visit a castle or stay in a hotel that has a ghost. Some people would even buy a wardrobe with a ghost in it …

# Chapter 1

# Mrs Rundle's Brainwave

Mr Rundle was eating his breakfast at the Dog and Duck inn. He drank a cup of tea, bit into his toast and looked at the adverts on the back page of the newspaper. Mrs Rundle sat on the other side of the table and read the headlines on the front page.

"I see the Chinese are sending an army of 300,000 troops to fight the Japanese," she said.

"Very nice, dear," Mr Rundle replied.

"I do wish you'd listen when I'm talking to you," Mrs Rundle snapped.

"Yes, I read all about that in the paper," Mr Rundle said.

Mrs Rundle leaned forward. "There is a great big spider crawling up your nose to eat your brain!" she said.

"Really, dear?"

"But it's run off again because it can't find any brains in there," she went on.

"Ah, that'll be all right, dear." Mr Rundle nodded and turned the page.

"I've put poison in your tea," Mrs Rundle said next.

"Good grief!" Mr Rundle yelled.

Mrs Rundle jumped. "I was only joking. I only said it to make you sit up and listen!"

"Would you believe it?" he shouted.

"Believe what?" Mrs Rundle said.

"It's Mrs Barclay!" he cried.

"What's she done now?"

"She's put an advert in the paper!"

"How exciting," Mrs Rundle said with a sigh.

"No, listen!  It says ...

"'FOR SALE – Wardrobe, with its own ghost.
I will be happy to deliver this to anyone who
wants to buy it.  The ghost will be more at
home if it is made to feel welcome.  Please
write to Mrs Barclay ...' and then it gives the
address."

"I always thought she was a funny woman,"
Mrs Rundle said.

"But you said she was a wonderful woman
and very charming, even though she was so
very rich.  Don't you remember?"  Mr Rundle

put down the newspaper and stuck his pipe in his mouth.

"Buy that wardrobe, Mr Rundle," his wife ordered.

Her husband opened his mouth and his pipe almost fell into his teacup. "What on earth for?"

"We want to make the Dog and Duck a bit smarter, don't we? It'll add interest to the place. People will come from miles around to stay in a room that has a wardrobe with a ghost in it," she told him. And she folded her fat arms.

"But where will we put it while we've got workmen in the Dog and Duck?" asked her husband.

"In the shed at the bottom of the garden. I'll phone Mrs Barclay now before someone else snaps it up," Mrs Rundle said. "You can do the washing-up."

# Chapter 2

# A Bargain Buy

Mrs Barclay was a small, neat woman. She wore a flowery dress and her grey hair was set in waves. She opened the door and her face lit up when she saw the Rundles.

"Oh, my dears, do come in!" she cried in a high voice.

"Do you have to open the door yourself, Mrs Barclay?" Mrs Rundle asked. "Where are all the servants?"

"We haven't got any!" Mrs Barclay said with a sigh. "They've all left because of the ghost. Even Martha, the cook, says she can't stand any more and she's off too. But come in and have a look at the wardrobe."

"It's a beautiful wardrobe," she went on as she led the way up the stairs. "I got it in a sale three years ago. It was just a normal wardrobe. But I liked it and bought it. Only cost me £10."

"Oh, Mr Rundle will give you £20," Mrs Rundle told her. "Won't you, Mr Rundle?"

"Why not make it £30?" her husband said rather crossly.

Mrs Barclay stopped at the top of the stairs. "I've had so many offers. First came the phone calls and today the letters began to arrive. I'll show them to you if you like. But have a look at the wardrobe first."

She led the way into the bedroom. Everything was very grand – the rich carpet, the pretty paper on the walls and the satin cover on the bed. But there was dust everywhere.

"You've lost your maids too, I see," Mrs Rundle said.

"Everyone has left and all because of the wardrobe!"

# Chapter 3

# Mrs Barclay's Story

They all looked at the wardrobe. It had drawers and mirrors and looked the same as any other wardrobe.

"It'll look nice in the best bedroom at the Dog and Duck," Mrs Rundle said with a smile.

"Everyone will want to see it," Mrs Barclay said with a laugh. "So many people want to buy it. You'll have lots more visitors."

"We never thought of that," said Mrs Rundle. But she was telling a fib.

"I'll show you some of my letters," Mrs Barclay went on. She led the way into the living room, sank into a chair and rang a bell. A woman with a white apron came out from the kitchen. She looked grumpy. "Tea for three, please, Martha," Mrs Barclay said.

Martha, the cook, went off to make it.

"We had no trouble for two years," Mrs Barclay said. "Then friends who stayed in that room began to ask about the wardrobe. Was there something odd about it? Why did the doors keep opening and shutting? Would we mind if they went home? Why, my dear, at this rate I'll have no friends left."

"Did you see anything yourself?" Mr Rundle asked.

"Oh, yes. Mr East – my butler – and I spent an evening there. We checked the wardrobe on the outside for secret panels and springs. Nothing! But when Mr East said he would look inside, something terrible happened. The door flew across the room and smashed into that mirror! We were scared stiff. I nearly fainted."

Mrs Rundle nodded. "I'd have died," she said.

"But we had woken up the ghost," Mrs Barclay went on.

"It had risen from the grave," Mrs Rundle added.

"Risen from the grave! That's just what Mr East said. Then, one night, a ghostly shape came out of the wardrobe ..."

# Chapter 4

# The Wardrobe Changes Hands

"How big was it?" Mr Rundle asked.

"Almost 8 foot tall," said Mrs Barclay.

"What!  A ghostly shape that is 8 foot tall!"

"No, no, the wardrobe is 8 foot tall," said Mrs Barclay.  "And the ghostly shape was about

five foot tall. It was a little old man with a
funny hat."

"What did this ghostly shape do?" Mr Rundle
asked.

"He walked downstairs and went out of the front door," Mrs Barclay told them.

"Ghosts walk through doors," Mr Rundle said. Everyone knew that.

"Well this one didn't," Mrs Barclay snapped. "He opened the door and slammed it behind him! Quite rude he was. Then the wardrobe doors kept opening and banging shut again. No one could get to sleep. The servants started to leave! The ghostly shape hated the butler and kicked him on the shins. He left too, of course."

"Can't blame him," Mr Rundle said.

"So the wardrobe has to go. Still, I never thought so many people would want it."

Mrs Barclay pointed to a table with letters sorted into neat piles on it. She walked across to the table and began to read the letters.

"Look at this one ...

Can I have my money back if the ghost
doesn't appear?

"And this ...

I am a professor of ghostly studies ...

"And this ...

We are four ladies living alone and we think the ghost might protect our house ...

"And this ...

Do you think your ghost would be happy in a small, modern house?

"The ghost might be happy in a modern house, but I don't think the wardrobe would fit. And look at this!" Mrs Barclay passed another letter to Mrs Rundle.

Mrs Rundle read it. She looked amazed. How very rude! She read it to her husband.

"Dear Mrs Barclay

I am very interested in your wardrobe and you. Will you marry me?"

"I've had lots of advice," Mrs Barclay went on.

**Don't lock the wardrobe …**

**Place a nice comfortable chair beside the wardrobe for the ghost.**

**There is almost certainly treasure inside …**

"And look at this," she said.

**If I were you I'd keep it.  You'll never have another wardrobe like that!**

"I ask you!"

Mrs Rundle put the letters back on the table.  "We'll buy the wardrobe, won't we, Harry dear?"

"Er … well …"

"Harry will give you £50, won't you, Harry dear?"

"Deal!" Mrs Barclay said. "I'll deliver it to you tomorrow. Some men from the newspapers want to spend the night in the room with the wardrobe first."

# Chapter 5

# Unwanted Visitors

A van pulled up at the Dog and Duck inn with three men in it. Mrs Barclay pulled up behind the van in her black Morris car.

Mrs Rundle looked on as the men carried the wardrobe to the shed at the bottom of the garden. "How did the newspaper men get on?" she asked.

"Most odd," Mrs Barclay said. "We had reporters from two local newspapers and one of the London papers too."

"Oooh!  You'll be famous!" Mrs Rundle told her.

"Well, they didn't want to take my photo," Mrs Barclay sniffed. "They only wanted photos of the wardrobe!"

"And did the little man come out?  The one in the funny hat?"

"Nothing happened for an hour," Mrs Barclay said in a low voice. "Then all at once there were sounds from inside the wardrobe. A reporter shone a torch on the floor and there was a button that had not been there before. Then I saw him. 'He's there!' I cried. The little man came out of the wardrobe and ran across the room."

"Did the reporters see him?" Mrs Rundle asked.

"No," Mrs Barclay said sadly. "They were too slow." She looked down the garden path of the Dog and Duck and saw the men close the shed door.

"Well, I see it's found a safe home," Mrs Barclay said. "I had so many offers ..."

"Oh! I mustn't forget to pay you," Mrs Rundle said and she pulled fifty £1 notes from her pocket.

"It would be cheap at twice the price," Mrs Barclay said, tucking the money away deep inside her handbag. "You'll see. You won't be able to move for visitors to the Dog and Duck now."

But, when the visitors came, they were not the sort the Rundles wanted.

# Chapter 6

# Ghostly Goings-on

The wardrobe at the bottom of the garden didn't bother the Rundles ... but the visitors did. Mr Rundle was filling a glass with beer behind the bar when a young man ran into the bar.

"The ghost!" he wailed. "There's a ghost out there! It's horrible. It's disgusting!"

The bar was full.  Everyone rushed to the door.  The young man had to move out of the way, fast.

Another young man was yelling, "The back garden.  The shed!  It came out of the shed wailing and screaming!"

The crowd from the bar pushed and shoved to be the first to see the ghost.  People in the same street came to their front doors to find out what was going on.  Soon there were fifty people standing in the back garden of the inn.

No one said a word.  In the silence a white shape came out of the shed.  It was tall and it flapped in the summer breeze.  Some people backed away.  Someone screamed.

The ghost began to make a sound that was … ghostly.

"Hoooo!  Hoooo!"

It had two large patches on the front of its head where eyes should have been. It turned to the crowd on the grass and began to move towards them. Even the brave ones began to panic as the cries of the crowd and the wails of the ghost grew louder.

Then the ghost tripped and fell forward. There was a ripping sound as the white sheet tore and the young man inside fell flat on his face. He was hooting with laughter!

"Caw!" he cried. "You should have seen your faces!"

The angry crowd moved towards him. He dashed down the garden, past the shed and over the wall that led to the railway line. He was still laughing as he ran off into the night.

# Chapter 7

# Things that Go Bump

"It's no good, Harry," one of the drinkers told Mr Rundle as they all went back inside the Dog and Duck. "You'll be the victim of every joker in the county as long as you have that thing in your shed."

Mr Rundle gave a sigh. "You're right. There's a room I can put it in upstairs. I'll bring it in first thing tomorrow."

But Mr and Mrs Rundle had a restless night. Stones rained down on the roof of their shed. Voices hooted through their letter-box. Screaming and howling went on all night. The police had to be called to get rid of the jokers.

Next morning Mr Rundle, with the help of some friends, dragged the wardrobe into the inn and up the stairs to the best bedroom.

The owners of the Dog and Duck looked forward to a restful night.

But that night Mr Rundle woke with a start. He was sure that he had heard a rumbling sound from the best bedroom. He slid his feet into an old pair of slippers and crept towards the door. The floor creaked under his feet, but his wife did not wake up. She was fast asleep and snoring.

Mr Rundle opened the bedroom door and it groaned like a dog with a sore tooth. There

was a little light from the moon.  Mr Rundle
wished he had a poker with him.

His mouth was dry.  He put his ear against
the door.  He heard the creaking noises that
the old inn often made in the night, but nothing
else.

When he pushed the door open something soft brushed against his face. He almost screamed with fear. But it was just a dressing gown hanging behind the door. The wardrobe was silent, but Mr Rundle felt it was the silence of an animal waiting to jump out at him.

He backed out of the room and padded back to bed. Was that the sound of laughter coming from the best bedroom?

# Chapter 8

# Peace at Last?

Mr Rundle tried to laugh about it next morning when he told his wife about the noises.

"I expect the ghost's looking for something," Mrs Rundle told her husband.

"Yes, dear," he replied.

"Take the wardrobe apart and you may find the treasure," she said.

"Yes, dear."

"Well?  What are you waiting for?"

"You want me to do it now?"

Mrs Rundle folded her arms.  Mr Rundle knew who was boss.  It took him an hour to take the wardrobe apart.  It took him two hours to put it back together again.

"No treasure," he told his wife.

And after that there was no ghost either. Perhaps the noises had driven the little old man in the funny hat away.

"£50 is a lot to pay for a plain old wardrobe," Mrs Rundle said a week later.  The fuss had died down and the visitors had stopped coming to see it.  "Why did you have to take it apart?" she asked.

"Sorry, dear," Mr Rundle said in a low voice.

Mr Rundle read his paper. "There's a nice wardrobe for sale here ..." he began.

Mrs Rundle folded her arms.

"Just a thought," her husband said with a sigh.

# Chapter 9

# Six Months Later

Some six months later Mr Rundle shut up the bar for the night. He wiped the last table clean and went into the kitchen to make his hot chocolate. Then he went upstairs. Mrs Rundle was staying with her sister that week. He had to work harder in the bar, but at least he had a bit of peace in the evening.

'Why not sleep in the best bedroom?' Mr Rundle thought. He slipped under the cool sheets and sipped his drink. He read the newspaper, then folded it and dropped it by the side of the bed. Then he wiped away the chocolate from round his mouth and turned off the light. He gave a sigh – he was a happy man. Only the faint light from a street lamp outside lit the room.

An owl hooted in the woods and a cat yowled in the garden.

A door creaked in the bedroom ...

Mr Rundle's eyes flew open. In the half-dark he saw the door of the wardrobe swing open. He saw a tweed jacket. It could have been his own jacket hanging there – or it could have belonged to the little old man with the funny hat.

Mr Rundle didn't stay to find out. He spent the night in the kitchen with the fire blazing and all the lights turned on.

When the sun rose and the first bus arrived in the village, his wife found him sitting at the table. There was a sheet of paper in his shaking hand. He'd written just three words –

"Ghost for sale ..."

# What do you think?

Was there a ghost?

The wardrobe had been mended at some time – a new panel had been filled into its floor. But perhaps the old one had been taken out to hide treasure, or perhaps the old one was rotten.

Had the ghost hidden something in the wardrobe when he was alive and put the new panel over it?

Had someone else found this hidden "something" and taken it away?

Was it money or was it treasure?

Is that why the grumpy little man with the funny hat came back night after night?

We can only guess.

Can you explain it?

Was Mrs Barclay telling fibs about her wardrobe? Remember, the newspaper men never saw her ghost. No one talked to her servants and asked them what they thought.

But why would Mrs Barclay want to lie about the ghost?

Here is one possible answer which fits the facts. But it has nothing to do with ghosts.

Perhaps Mrs Barclay needed money. A lot of rich people lost a lot of their money in the

1930s.  One by one Mrs Barclay's servants left because she couldn't pay their wages.

She thought up a plan to make money.  It would bring her some cash – and it would also explain to everyone why such a "rich" woman had no servants.

So, Mrs Barclay buys ten old wardrobes for £5 each.  She puts an advert for a wardrobe "with its own ghost" in the newspaper.  She has lots of offers.  Many people are willing to pay £50 (or more) for what is just a piece of junk – if they get a ghost with it.  She sells the ten wardrobes to the ten best offers.

"This is the one and only wardrobe with its own ghost," she tells each person who buys a wardrobe.

Result?  Mrs Barclay makes nearly £500.

Possible?  What do you think?

Our books are tested
for children and young people by
children and young people.

Thanks to everyone who consulted on
a manuscript for their time and effort in
helping us to make our books better
for our readers.

# Also by *Terry Deary* ...

"Ahoy there me hearties!"

That's pirate speak, as you know. We salty sea-dogs use it to set us apart from the landlubbers.

It's time to pull on your sea-boots and join Roger Redbeard and his pirate crew as they set sail across the Spanish Main – or at least their local park – in search of long-lost treasure.

A game of two halves ...

Jud's team is 2–0 down in the big match
when their star player is hurt.

Can Jud save the day?

www.barringtonstoke.co.uk